Paul Granite
Renik
28/11

Illustrations by Hsin-Shih Lai
Book design by Howard Kirk Besserman
Based on the English translation by Margaret Hunt

Published by Bell Pond Books
610 Main Street, Great Barrington, MA 01230

www.bellpondbooks.com

ISBN 978-0-88010-583-5
Library of Congress Cataloging-in-Publication Data is available.
Printed in the United States of America

ENCHANTMINTS DESIGN STUDIO

THE
BREMEN TOWN
MUSICIANS

BY THE BROTHERS GRIMM

ILLUSTRATIONS BY HSINSHIH LAI

BOOK DESIGN BY HOWARD KIRK BESSERMAN

A certain man had a donkey, who had carried the corn sacks to the mill tirelessly for many years.

Now the donkey was growing old, and as his strength left him he became more and more unfit for work. And so his master began to think of turning him out.

But the donkey guessed that misfortune was in the wind and ran away, taking the road to Bremen. "There," he thought "I can surely be a town musician."

When he had walked some distance, he found a hound lying by the road, panting as if he had just run a long way. "Why are you gasping so, old fellow?" asked the donkey.

"Ah," replied the hound, "as I am weak, and no longer swift enough to hunt, my master wanted to kill me, so I ran away. But now how am I to earn my bread?"

"I tell you what," said the donkey, "I am going to Bremen, to be town musician there. Come with me and be a musician too. I will play the lute, and you can beat the kettle-drum." The hound agreed, and on they went.

Before long they came to a cat sitting on the path, with a grim and downcast face. "Friend, you look gloomier than a rainy day," said the donkey. "Why are you sad?"

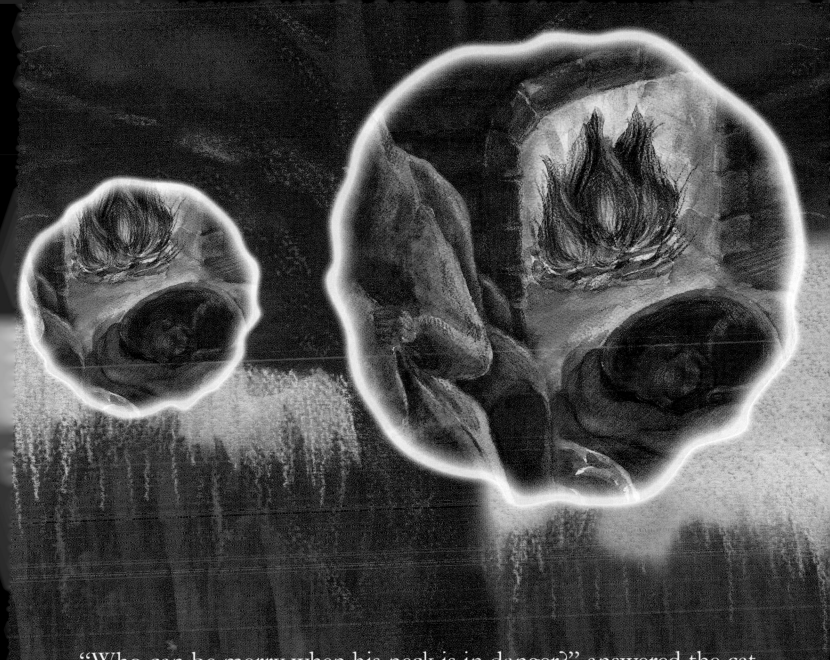

"Who can be merry when his neck is in danger?" answered the cat. "Because I am getting old, and my teeth are worn to stumps, and I prefer to sit by the fire rather than hunt for mice, my mistress wanted to drown me, so I ran away. But now good advice is scarce. Where am I to go?"

"Go with us to Bremen. You understand serenading. You can be a town musician."

The cat agreed and went with them.

After this, the three fugitives came to a farmyard, where
a rooster was sitting upon the gate, crowing with all
his might. "Your crowing goes through and
through me, right to my bones," said the
donkey. "What is the matter?"

"I am foretelling fine weather
because it is the day Our Lady
washes the Christ-child's
little shirts and hangs
them up to dry,"
said the
rooster.

"But guests are coming for Sunday dinner, so the farmer's wife has no pity. I heard her tell the cook that she intends to eat me in the soup tomorrow. This very evening I am to have my head cut off. Now I am crowing at the top of my lungs while I still can."

"Ah, but red-comb," said the donkey, "you had better come away with us. We are going to Bremen, to be town musicians. You have a good voice, and surely we will make fine music together."

The rooster agreed to this plan, and all four went on together.

At evening they came to a forest. The travelers were still a long way from Bremen, so they stopped among the trees to take shelter for the night. The donkey and the hound laid themselves down at the foot of a large tree, the cat settled himself in the branches, and the rooster flew to the very top, where he felt safest.

Before he went to sleep he looked around in all four directions,
and thought he saw in the distance a little spark burning.
So he called out to his companions that there must be a
house not far off, with a light in its window.

The donkey said, "If so, we had better get up
and go on, for the shelter here is bad."
The hound thought too that a few
bones with some meat on them
would do him good.

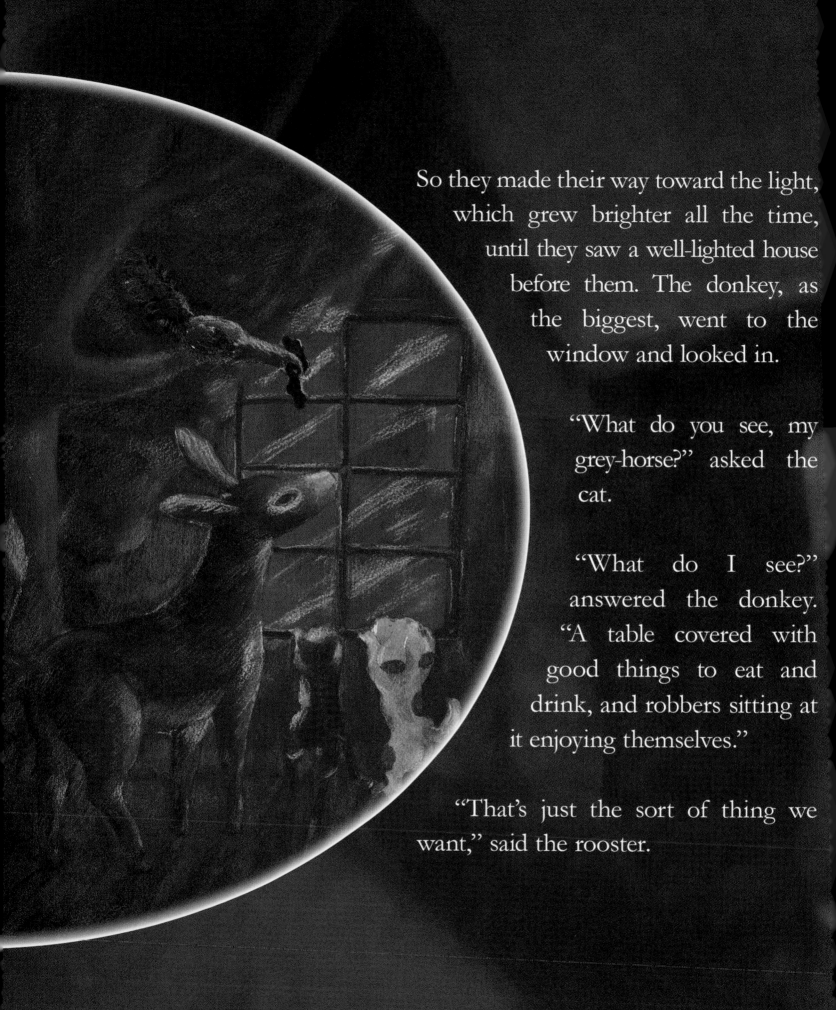

So they made their way toward the light, which grew brighter all the time, until they saw a well-lighted house before them. The donkey, as the biggest, went to the window and looked in.

"What do you see, my grey-horse?" asked the cat.

"What do I see?" answered the donkey. "A table covered with good things to eat and drink, and robbers sitting at it enjoying themselves."

"That's just the sort of thing we want," said the rooster.

Then the animals thought together how they might drive away the robbers, until they came up with a plan. First, the donkey placed his forefeet on the window ledge. Then the hound jumped on the donkey's back. The cat climbed upon the hound, and finally the rooster flew up and perched upon the cat's head.

All at once they began to perform their music together. The donkey brayed, the hound barked, the cat mewed, and the rooster crowed. Then they burst through the window into the room, shattering the glass.

At this horrible din, the robbers sprang
up, thinking that a ghost had come in, and
fled in a great fright out into the forest.

The four companions now sat down at the table, well content with what was left, and ate as if they were going to fast for a month.

As soon as the four minstrels had eaten, they put out the light, and each found a sleeping place that suited him. The donkey laid down upon some straw in the yard, the hound stretched out behind the door, the cat curled up on the hearth near the warm ashes, and the rooster perched upon a beam of the roof. And, being tired from their long walk, they soon went to sleep.

When it was
past midnight, and
the robbers saw from their
hiding place that the light was no
longer burning in their house and all
appeared quiet, the captain said, "We ought not
to have let ourselves be frightened out of our wits."
Then he ordered one of them to go and examine the house.

The messenger, finding all was still, went into the kitchen to light a candle. Taking the fiery eyes of the cat for live coals, he held a match to them to light it.

But the cat did not understand the joke and sprang at the robber's face, spitting and scratching. The robber was dreadfully frightened and ran to the back door, but the hound, who was lying there, sprang up and bit his leg. And as he ran across the yard by the dunghill, the donkey gave him a smart kick with his hind foot. The rooster, too, who had been awakened by the noise, cried down from the beam, "Cock-a-doodle-doo!"

The robber ran back as
fast as he could to his captain,
crying, "Help, help! There is a horrible witch
sitting in the house, who spat on me and scratched
my face with her long claws. And by the door stands a
man with a knife, who stabbed me in the leg. And in the
yard lies a black monster, who beat me with a wooden club.
And above, on the roof, sits the judge, who called out, 'Bring
that troublemaker here to me!' I was lucky to escape with my life!"

After this the
robbers never again
dared enter the house. But
it suited the four musicians
of Bremen so well that
they did not care to
leave it any more.

THE END